"One of Mexico's best-known novelists . . . Bellatin is usually included in a group of post-boom Latin American writers, such as the Chilean Roberto Bolaño and the Argentine César Aira, who have introduced innovations not only in the style of their prose but in the way they think about literature. In Bellatin's stories, the line between reality and fiction is blurry; the author himself frequently appears as a character. His books are fragmentary, their atmospheres bizarre, even disturbing. They are full of mutations, fluid sexual identities, mysterious diseases, deformities." — *The New Yorker*

"People often say, with a lot of truth to it, that all good fiction writing comes from some wound, out of some distance that needs to be breached between a writer and normalcy. In Mario's sense, the wound is literal and comes with all kinds of psychological nuance and pain, and seems related to sexuality and desire, the desire for a whole body. One of my favorite aspects of him is this sense that he is writing for all the freaks — either literally freaks or privately and metaphorically, that he really touches us." — Francisco Goldman

"Bellatin offers a different way of reading, and of telling, a story — one in which what is unsaid, incompletely rendered, allows respectful room for discovering and conveying more than we might have imagined, or were told that we could."
— *Words Without Borders*

MRS. MURAKAMI'S GARDEN

ALSO AVAILABLE IN ENGLISH BY MARIO BELLATIN

Beauty Salon
(translated by David Shook)

Flowers & Mishima's Illustrated Biography
(translated by Kolin Jordan)

Jacob the Mutant
(translated by Jacob Steinberg)

The Large Glass
(translated by David Shook)

Shiki Nagaoka: A Nose for Fiction
(translated by David Shook)

The Transparent Bird's Gaze
(translated by David Shook)

MRS. MURAKAMI'S GARDEN
Oto no-Murakami monogatari

Mario Bellatin

Translated from the Spanish by

Heather Cleary

Deep Vellum Publishing
Dallas, Texas

Deep Vellum Publishing
3000 Commerce St., Dallas, Texas 75226
deepvellum.org · @deepvellum

Deep Vellum is a 501c3 nonprofit literary arts organization
founded in 2013 with the mission to bring
the world into conversation through literature.

Support for this publication has been provided in part by grants from the
National Endowment for the Arts, the Texas Commission on the Arts, the City
of Dallas Office of Arts and Culture's ArtsActivate program, and the Moody
Fund for the Arts:

978-1-64605-029-1 (paperback) | 978-1-64605-030-7 (ebook)

LIBRARY OF CONGRESS CONTROL NUMBER: 2020945030

Cover Artwork & Design by Justin Childress | justinchildress.co
Interior Layout and Typesetting by KGT

PRINTED IN THE UNITED STATES OF AMERICA

Mrs. Izu Murakami's garden would soon be dismantled, its great black and white stones removed. Its streams would be drained, along with the pond at its center, now filled with golden carp. Mrs. Murakami used to sit by that pond for hours on end, watching the flashes of fin and scale. She abandoned this pastime when she became a widow. The house was sealed off from the world, its windows shuttered. But the garden retained its splendor. The care of the residence was left to the elderly servant Shikibu. The garden was tended by an experienced old man hired by Mrs. Murakami to check on it twice a week.

Late some afternoons, at the hour when shadows blur the contours of things, Mrs. Murakami thinks she sees her husband's silhouette across the pond. Now and then she senses him waving to her, so she sits on one of the stones along the path and squints toward the far end of the garden. These visions only appear under favorable atmospheric conditions. Once, she watched the ghost sink feet first into one of the streams.

Her husband's death was a terrible ordeal. He spent his final days in a state of delirium, calling for none other than Etsuko, his wife's former *saikoku*.[1] He wanted to see her breasts again. At first, Mrs. Murakami tried not to hear him. She ignored the dying man's pleas and sought to maintain her composure at his side. Only Shikibu noticed the faint blush that rose to her cheeks, especially when her husband mentioned Etsuko in front of the doctor.

Mrs. Murakami allowed no visitors during her husband's illness. Not even the friends he dined with once a week were admitted into their home. To vent some of the anger provoked by Mr. Murakami's outrageous behavior, she went out to the garden while the others prepared the body of the recently deceased, and she pulled up the

---

1. See footnote 5.

bamboo he had planted at their housewarming. It was real bamboo. Mr. Murakami had purchased the tiny stalks during the Festival of Lanterns, on the night he'd asked for her hand in marriage. Her rage went unnoticed by the employees of the funeral home. Shikibu closed the aluminum shutters on the doors and windows overlooking the garden. Then she tried to calm her mistress. She suggested a bath with wild herbs, and prepared the *kimono*[2] she would wear for the ceremony. It was the lavender *kimono* Mrs. Murakami had worn to her wedding. On its back were two blue herons in flight. The *obi*[3] chosen to go with it was bright red. While the others prepared her master for the funeral, Shikibu carefully did Mrs. Murakami's hair. It was a complex style. Mrs. Murakami found it ostentatious and thought that not even her husband's oldest friends would recognize her done up like that. She worried what they might think. Shikibu consoled her with gentle words and convinced her that her reputation was unblemished, despite the circumstances.

---

2. Traditional garment typically made by women.
3. A belt, the measurements of which are based on images of Shinto goddesses.

The funeral was held on a beautiful day. The sun lit the garden with uncommon intensity. The white stones looked whiter than usual and the black stones absorbed the light, taking on a matte finish. Before leaving for the ceremony, Mrs. Murakami walked along one of the garden's streams and caught sight of the pond out of the corner of her eye. The fins and tails of the koi sparkled as if illuminated from within. She would have liked to stay there, watching the fish, but her husband's black car was waiting for her out front.

Mr. Murakami owned a black car produced after the war. It had been assigned to a foreign colonel who'd hardly used it before being unexpectedly transferred out of the country. His friends reproached him for his ostentatious purchase, given the current state of affairs. Nor did they look kindly on doing business with the foreign troops. Mr. Murakami simply smiled at these criticisms and said, in his defense, that the others would soon be emulating him. He was right: his friends quickly abandoned their qualms about displaying their wealth in public.

Mrs. Murakami had unpleasant memories of that

car. Early in their courtship, her future husband would send his driver to her home with expensive offerings. Mrs. Murakami — at that time, still just Izu — would watch him park at their gate from her window. The first was a gift of black orchids grown on the islands west of their country. Her father's illness had taken a turn for the worse. He spent most of the day in bed. Her suitor was a widower a good deal older than her, but Izu was about to turn twenty-five. The family was in no position to turn him down. It was common knowledge that they were eager to marry off their daughter. Two young men had already asked for her hand, but unfortunate circumstances had prevented both weddings. The first suitor, Akira, had died of rabies. One afternoon he was bitten by a small dog that ran up to him as he left his fiancée's house. Akira left the wound on his right leg untended. He forgot all about the incident and died two months later from nervous fits. The second suitor, Tutzio, took a trip before the wedding and no one heard from him again. He was going to spend some time in America. He wanted to visit his brothers before marrying, to explore the possibility of moving there with his new wife. The truth was that he wanted to ask forgiveness for the way he'd behaved the last time he was there.

One year later, Izu heard a rumor that, before he had even arrived in San Francisco, his brothers had arranged for him to marry the daughter of a man who owned a chain of Asian restaurants.

After these failures, Izu decided to forget about marriage and dedicate herself with greater discipline to her studies. She pursued a degree in art history at one of the best universities in the city with the aim of becoming a distinguished critic. She met Mr. Murakami, in fact, while working on a paper. Mr. Murakami had a prestigious, though not particularly large, collection of traditional artwork in his home. Many of the objects dated back ten centuries. The friends he dined with once a week declared part of the house a museum, christening it The Murakami. He had inherited most of the pieces from his father, who got rich the century before by doing business outside the country. His interests, however, were not only commercial: his taste for a wide range of artistic forms could be traced back to his youth. He always found time to see a *kabuki*[4] performance or to spend days in museums and antique shops. He never studied art, but

---

4. A style of theater performed only by men, in which there is no synchronization between speech and movement.

he seemed to have a gift for recognizing valuable pieces on the spot. Because of this aptitude, it was only a few years before specialists began discussing his collection. The businessman instilled in his son a passion for this legacy. He bequeathed the house and all its contents to him. Before his father died, the son promised to continue to build the collection until it was the most important in the country. He was not, however, able to keep his word. Everything was fine while he was married to the honorable and sickly Shosatsu, and even during his years as a widower. But that all changed when he met Izu.

Izu paid a visit to Mr. Murakami one morning in early December. Though it had not snowed the night before, there was a dryness in the air that usually follows a snowfall. She was accompanied by Etsuko, her faithful servant.[5] She'd arranged the meeting one week in advance. Mr. Murakami himself had answered the phone. The following Thursday, a few days before the appointment, he

5. A *saikoku*, really, as the role was understood in imperial times: something between a servant, a housekeeper, and a chaperone. *Saikokus* performed all these functions and, at the same time, none.

told his friends that he'd been pleasantly surprised by the timbre in the voice of the woman who'd asked to see his collection. When he saw her, Mr. Murakami was unusually friendly. He later confessed to thinking he had seen something of his late wife in her. Izu was wearing a traditional dark green *kimono* with a black *obi*. It was one of those that had been produced during the Repression.[6] It was not decorated with embroidered patterns or reliefs. In that period, tailors developed a remarkable form of craftsmanship: they needed to employ all their talent without ever letting it show. Etsuko stayed two steps behind him, wearing a kimono her mistress had lent to her. Mr. Murakami sent his housekeepers away and showed the pieces himself. He did, however, allow his servant Shikibu to stay. He quietly asked her to attend to anything they might need. The elderly servant greeted Izu with mistrust, but extended her the same courtesy that every guest received. The tour lasted almost four hours. The objects were illuminated by small alcohol lamps set high on the walls. Izu wondered who lit them, since the

---

6. Time of military rule between the Meiji and Kamakura periods, during which all personal adornments were considered an homage to the former imperial powers.

people in charge of lighting the city's streets and houses that way had disappeared years earlier. On this occasion, Mr. Murakami was especially detailed in his description of the objects. Afterward he invited his guest to stay for tea. He praised Shikibu's skill at preparing the drink. While they would not be having a formal tea ceremony, Shikibu had devised a method for drinking tea according to tradition in less than half an hour. She filled a metal pot with water and placed it on the stove. While the water boiled, the elderly servant selected the right cups for the occasion and placed in each a small paper satchel containing the dried leaves of the tea plant. Next, she would take the water off the burner and pour it into the cups, which she would then cover with the same small plates she would later rest them on. She would wait five minutes, and then remove the satchels from the cups. The final step consisted of putting the cups on a ceramic platter, along with a little plate of thinly sliced lemon and a sugar bowl with a silver spoon that complemented the platter. As Izu smiled and declined the invitation, she put away the notebook in which she'd written her thoughts and said a friendly goodbye. Etsuko followed her out of the house. When he met with his friends the following

Thursday, Mr. Murakami remarked that he only noticed the servant's presence as they were saying goodbye.

In the days that followed, Izu was busy with her assignments for the university, especially the composition of an essay about her recent visit to Mr. Murakami's collection. Her intention had been to underscore the relationship it established between past and present. She noticed, however, historical biases she felt she should mention, certain imbalances in the selection of work. Perhaps these subtle errors revealed a lack of academic training. She had no choice but to be tough in her appraisal of the criteria applied. It was inexcusable, she thought, that works were selected in certain periods according to dynasty, and simply according to their utilitarian or military value in others. The exhibit seemed thrown together, she declared, according to the whim of someone who suddenly found himself in a position to satisfy any desire he might have.

Izu's essay startled her professor. His name was Matsuei Kenzo and his body was chiseled, as if he spent all his free time at the gym or a nearby *shojibo.*[7] Some

---

7. Establishments that made their clients feel as if they were at the beach. These were very popular in the sixties.

of the girls at the university were in love with him and flocked to his classes just to be near him. Nonetheless, no one had ever heard rumors of an affair. This made him even more admirable in the eyes of Izu, who would never take a class with anyone whose behavior was not above reproach. She hated the way her classmates would whisper among themselves and make irrelevant comments, but she attended lecture anyway. Master Matsuei Kenzo declared her essay truthful and daring. He told her that such work was uncommon in their country. It was not unusual elsewhere, where aesthetic and intellectual opinions were not necessarily tied to personal matters. It was conceivable, he continued, that somewhere else one could write a scathing review of the work of an artist friend and the friendship would continue as before. Her professor had been so surprised by her paper that he suggested publishing it in an art magazine to which he had ties. If the idea interested her, she should submit an abridged version.

The cold weather those days suggested that the coming winter would be a harsh one. Izu was in the habit of attending classes in Western attire. On that occasion, she was wearing a beige cashmere sweater, a kilt fastened with a large safety pin, and a pair of flats that could be adorned with a coin. To walk around campus, she put on a long lambswool coat. She was excited about Master Matsuei Kenzo's comments, and even more so about the idea of publishing her essay. There were two competing factions at the university: the Radical Conservatives, led by the diminutive Master Takagashi, and Adamantly Modern, the group to which Master Matsuei Kenzo belonged. The Radical Conservatives had controlled the department since its creation. They wanted to protect their ancestral past without the incursion of foreign ideas or contemporary techniques for preserving the country's cultural patrimony. Before meeting Etsuko, who picked her up from the university every day, Izu ran into two of her classmates. Both were slim, had longish hair, and wore glasses with square frames. They were talking about something unusual they'd seen in the Arts and Culture section of the newspaper that morning. It was an article about a man who vomited on famous works of art. The individual would gorge himself on pineapple or strawberries and would then spray the pieces with a layer of yellow or red vomit, depending on the fruit. The law was on his side wherever he committed this act, as it was impossible to prove intentionality. Izu remained standing as she listened to them. Then she told them she was in a rush.

Izu had a room in her parents' house where she could dedicate herself to her studies. They'd set up the small space, which had once been used for tea ceremonies, when she started at the university. It looked out over a little garden, which, though lovely, paled in comparison to the one she would enjoy after she married. Sometimes Izu would ask Etsuko to bring her *futon*[8] into the study and would sleep there rather than in the main room, with the rest of the family. A pair of sliding doors connected the study to the garden. These were opened or closed depending on the weather. On warm, sunny days, the doors were left wide open and an intense light would bathe her books, notebooks, and Olivetti typewriter. A little stream passed through the garden. The ground was sloped, however, so fish never spent much time there. She had to settle for the sound of the water and the cool breeze that sometimes filtered in.

---

8. A mattress of pressed cotton that provides warmth in the cold and, conversely, a cooling sensation when the weather gets hot.

Two days after Master Matsuei Kenzo's pronouncement, Izu began abridging her essay for publication in the magazine. Night was about to fall. A cold wind blew in from the south, making it hard to see beyond the garden. The doors and windows were closed. Izu had put on a thick *kimono* and wool stockings. She had no plans to go out. She'd returned home from the university an hour earlier and her only responsibility, aside from the commissioned article, was to put her father to bed. The three women of the house moved him every evening from the *tatami*[9] to the *futon* where he slept. Once he was settled in, her mother would leave a small towel beside his bed for his morning exercises. Before she went to bed, Izu was supposed to repeat the prayers of the monk Magetsu. Her father and entire family were followers. According to legend, it was Magetsu[10] who invented the game of three white

9. A mat woven from soft rush frequently used to cover the floor. Tatamis come in one size only, so rooms are often measured by how many fit inside.

10. A fundamentalist monk who claimed to have had not one, but many deaths. Upon each of these demises he made alarming prophecies that have not yet proved accurate. His following is widespread, especially in mountainous regions.

stones against three black stones, which for centuries was played only in secret. As she prayed, Izu massaged her father's feet according to the principles of *shiatsu*[11] she had learned from a manual.

Izu performed a different treatment on her father in the mornings. The doctor had shown her how. Each session lasted an hour and a half. As soon as she got up, she would walk over to where her ailing father slept, her gaze fixed on his closed eyelids. She would place her right hand on his forehead and blow gently on his face. That was when her mother, who slept on a *futon* nearby, would usually wake up. Without even stretching, she would get up to help her daughter. It was strange to see her at that hour, with her long gray hair disheveled. She had to hold her husband up by the arms so Izu could massage around his neck. Izu pressed in with one finger while the same finger on the other hand steadied his clavicle. She worked on the area for nearly an hour. The women did not know whether he enjoyed these massages or not. The patient never seemed to be awake during the treatment. At the most, every now and then

---

11. A form of curative massage.

the old man would emit a series of sounds that neither mother nor daughter ever managed to decipher. Other times, it would be an endless trail of saliva, which Izu's mother wiped away with the small towel she left next to his *futon* for that purpose. At the end of this process, the two women moved Izu's father to the *tatami* where he spent his days.

The first sign of Mr. Murakami came one week after Izu visited his collection of traditional art. At nine in the morning, after Izu had finished her father's treatment and was getting ready to go to class, the black car parked in front of her gate. The driver got out, knocked on the door, and dropped a bouquet of black orchids into Etsuko's arms. "For the sound that breathed life into the collection," read the note. The next day, Izu received a call from one of the women who worked at the exhibition, inviting her to dinner at a restaurant downtown on behalf of Mr. Murakami. She declined. A prior engagement. Then she went to her study and stood near the windows that looked out over the garden. She opened them, despite the cold. To take in the frozen air. She thought about the most recent draft of her article. Discretion had led her to cut several of its most biting critiques. She walked over to her desk without closing the windows and sat, shuffling papers. Five minutes later, she had begun to type. She was rewriting her original critiques.

The gifts continued to flow in the days that followed. From Etsuko's hands, Izu received perfume, handcrafted carvings commemorating the many deaths of the monk Magetsu, strange flowers, and catalogs of traditional art. These objects were always accompanied by a card alluding to Izu's voice. In one of his messages, Mr. Murakami even went so far as to compare it to the voice of the goddess Tamabe, who, with just two trills, had made the heavens release the first grains of rice. No one had ever paid much attention to Izu's voice. Except for the time when a winner of the game of three white stones against three black stones presented her with the ribbon he'd worn in the match. He said it was for the angelic cheering he'd heard during the showdown, to which he attributed his win. After weeks of these gifts, Mr. Murakami sent a gold bracelet. Izu was shaken by its arrival. She didn't want her mother to see it, so she locked herself in the bathroom. Once she was alone, she tried the bracelet on and observed how it looked against her forearm for nearly half an hour. Izu's skin was light brown, and the contours of her arms were unique to women from Ochun.[12] Her coloring and unusual physiognomy revealed her mixed lineage. Her father was of warrior stock from the middle of the country, while her mother was from the small islands of the archipelago. Izu's appearance had drawn attention ever since she was a child. She had been conscious of this all her life, but it bothered her to be praised for her looks alone. She was always trying to prove that what really mattered was her determination.

When she had stared at the bracelet long enough, she ordered Etsuko to return it the following weekend. She wrapped it back up carefully so no one could tell she'd opened it. Etsuko obeyed, walking alone to Mr. Murakami's house that Saturday. Izu took great pains to make sure she was presentable. She dressed her in a modestly elegant *kimono*. Etsuko gradually left the house behind, the package in her hands. She was gone for hours. Izu waited for her anxiously. She wanted to know

---

12. A region set squarely in the middle of the country, which produces women known for having remarkably well-delineated figures.

how Mr. Murakami had taken her rebuff. The delay made her think that perhaps there had been an accident. When Etsuko finally returned, she seemed paler than usual. When asked what had taken her so long, Etsuko replied that Mr. Murakami hadn't been home and that she had waited for hours in the entryway. Izu had more questions for her, but Etsuko went to bed without saying another word.

The article was published in January—surprisingly quickly, given that its author was unknown. A few days later, the gifts stopped appearing at her door. Izu waited a week before calling Mr. Murakami. She wanted to apologize for returning the bracelet, and to thank him for his generosity. The same woman who had relayed her dinner invitation picked up the phone. She said that no one was home, but that she would be sure to give Mr. Murakami the message personally. Mr. Murakami did not return her call. Izu tried again the following week. She spoke with the same woman, who again told her that her employer was not home. Mr. Murakami did not call her back this time, either.

•

The next day, after her classes, Izu stopped by Master Matsuei Kenzo's cubicle. She wanted to know if there had been any fallout from the article's publication. The professor told her that he had just spoken with the director of the art magazine where her article had appeared. As far as they could tell, there hadn't been. This was strange, because the targets of that kind of critique typically would take out ads in the newspapers to challenge the opinions presented. Master Matsuei Kenzo also told her that the director of the magazine was very pleased with her critique. "Finally, someone dared to unmask a fraud whose collection rests on the most obsolete criteria," were his exact words. It had never been her intention to unmask anyone, Izu thought, but she was glad the director was happy with her work. Before leaving, she asked her professor how she might collect her fee.

The magazine's director was named Mizoguchi Aori. At the suggestion of Master Matsuei Kenzo, Izu went to see him the following week. She wore a coat with fabric-covered buttons. It was early February and the afternoon was so cold that she'd put on dark gloves and a pair of tinted eyeglasses to avoid the winter sun. She took these off when she entered the reception area, sliding them up into her hair. The magazine's offices were pleasant. The furnishings had clean lines and were topped with Formica.[13] The entryway was flanked by two floor lamps on dimmers and a pair of miniature palm trees. Reproductions of traditional and modern artworks hung on the walls. The director wore black. He was around thirty years old and was beginning to go bald. He had a Great Dane with him that spent the entire time curled up on the carpet in a corner of his office. The only thing on the walls in there were reproductions of paintings by Francis Bacon.[14] Director Mizoguchi Aori received Izu personally. After welcoming her, he said that her article was very brave. He also mentioned that they were all unsettled by the silence that had followed its publication. All Mizoguchi Aori knew was that Mr. Murakami had been the object of subtle teasing from his friends at their weekly dinner last Thursday. He had been somber throughout the meal, offering no sign of the obliging

---

13. A synthetic material used predominantly by the furniture industry, though it can also be used in interior design. Among its virtues are its ability to resemble finer materials like wood or marble, and how easy it is to clean.

14. An English painter.

attitude he'd shown those same friends when they had criticized him for buying the black car or doing business with the occupying troops.

Izu began to regret her behavior. Something made her suspect she'd been too hasty. It wasn't even her idea, she thought. It was Master Matsuei Kenzo who had assigned her a paper on the Murakami collection. In the classes leading up to the assignment, he had spoken about the danger posed by amateur collectors. Without any training, they dared to set the rules for the art world, he argued. Seated in her study, trying to concentrate on a paper she needed to turn in the next day, Izu searched her heart for the real reasons behind her critique. She typed furiously on her Olivetti. Mr. Murakami was stocky, with short arms and legs. He was bald, and his head was almost perfectly round. A few hairs he'd clearly forgotten to trim the morning they met peeked out from his slightly pointed ears. For a moment, Izu saw in Mr. Murakami the pitiful best option she could hope for at that point. Time was passing her by. It seemed like not long ago that her father had taken her every Saturday to watch the game of three white stones against three back stones in the basement of the family's business. She suddenly felt that her life had been somewhat empty. She was twenty-five years old and, though it had not been her intention, she now had a vaguely shameful memory to look back on.

Izu was getting ready to start at the university when her first suitor, Akira, died. She had put off her studies because of her father's illness, and many of her grade school classmates already had careers by the time she made up her mind to go. The couple agreed that she would attend university after they married. Akira's parents emphatically opposed the idea. They had never liked her and didn't want their son marrying an intellectual. At the funeral, they refused to seat her according to her rank. Instead, Izu sat with the distant relatives of the deceased. After the cremation, she wasn't given even one of the bones that she was due. The afternoon Akira died, Izu was coming back from the home of Mr. Mitsubishi, who gave private lessons on how to pass university entrance exams. Her mother was waiting for her in the doorway. When she saw Izu, she rushed to meet her. Izu thought that something must have happened to her father. His illness had grown quite serious by then. Though he wasn't yet spending his days on the *tatami*, he was having trouble moving around the house. "Progressive deterioration of the lymphatic system," had been the doctor's pronouncement. The process would eventually kill the patient when the symptoms reached his lungs. When Izu asked what was going on, her mother burst into tears, covering her face with both hands. "Your boyfriend has rabies. They say there's no hope," she said and hurried inside. Her mother's words left Izu with the sensation that she was floating. She slipped into a rapture. When the news finally sank in, she set off running for Akira's house. There were cars parked outside. She was still carrying the notebooks where she'd written down Master Mitsubishi's lessons. She hadn't been able to see Akira at all that week, her studies had kept her too busy. She'd called her boyfriend twice, but his parents had refused to put him on the phone. They had said that he was under the weather and couldn't get up to take her call. As Izu entered the house, a doctor walked out, accompanied by two nurses. A woman standing next to the door informed her that visitors were not allowed beyond the vestibule. The woman had styled her hair strangely and was wearing a pink sweater. Izu thought she recognized her. Months later, she would remember that it was

Akira's aunt, and would speculate that she had styled her hair that way before learning of her nephew's ordeal. The woman told her that the doctor had ordered a complete disinfection before the body could be removed. Izu felt an intense heat spread across her back. She did not say a word at the funeral. Throughout the entire ceremony, Izu kept thinking that she needed to go home to study for the entrance exam. If she passed, her parents had promised to convert the room used for tea ceremonies into a study where she could dedicate herself to her intellectual pursuits. She also tried to remember the lessons that Master Mitsubishi had taught her over the past few days. When it was time to go, Etsuko was waiting for her at the entrance to the temple.

Izu met her second suitor during her third semester at the university. Tutzio's family had already spoken with her parents. They were concerned about their youngest son's bachelorhood. His brothers lived in the United States and Tutzio had spent a few years there, himself. He had poetic tendencies and, encouraged by his literary friends, had traveled to Mexico to experience things his family could not describe in precise terms. His brothers had sent him home, telling his parents that he would only be allowed to visit again if he made the journey with his wife, ready to start a business. Izu's parents were told only that the family wanted to find a wife for the young man. The prospect did not bother Izu. She had always been attracted to men who had traveled to the West and were able to combine the best of both cultures. Still, she had only known him for a few days before she began to find his behavior strange. Tutzio always seemed bored around her. The only thing her betrothed would do when he visited her study was to call his parents at home, repeatedly, to tell them he was with her. He also told her about Dazai Osamu, whom he considered to be the only real writer of that century. Izu rushed out to buy his books and read them in secret. The stories seemed very sad. At one point, she expressed her opinion. Tutzio did not respond. He also said nothing when she outlined the real history of their country's art as it had been taught to her by her university professors, as opposed to the version spread by scholars on the government's payroll. They spent every afternoon together. He disappeared at sundown, but not before pressing Izu against the bushes beside the front gate, where he boldly touched her. When Tutzio announced, a few weeks before the wedding, that he was going to San Francisco to prepare their future life there, Izu sensed she would not see him again. Before leaving, he gave her a symbolic gift: a small box containing the stump of his umbilical cord.[15] He also promised her that he would buy an *otsu*[16] where they could be buried together. After Tutzio left, his mother began to visit Izu every day for a few hours. She seemed to be trying to make up for her son's absence. A year later, Izu's mother finally asked her not to return. She was very polite about it, saying that her daughter needed to dedicate that time to her studies.

The call she hoped to receive from Mr. Murakami did not come in the following days. As usual, Izu dedicated her time to her studies and to her father's care. The family

---

15. The gift of an umbilical cord is a deep-seated tradition in the country, particularly among the entrepreneurial class. In many cases it serves as the engagement.

16. A measure of land typically found in cemeteries. An otsu is approximately half a square meter; as a result, the dead are often buried feet first.

owned a few department stores downtown. Years earlier, her father had helped run the business. Then his brothers took over, depositing his share of the profits in the bank for him every month. Despite all the money they had spent on doctors and medicines, there was no sign of economic trouble in the household. It seemed Izu's father had been prudent enough that he could now weather any storm without having to worry. Izu was financially stable, but she wanted a job outside the house. Her classes were usually in the morning, which left her afternoons free. She was looking for work because the university had started to feel a bit narrow for her interests. She had wanted to participate in the outside world ever since she was a child. When she was eleven, she wrote a treatise on the game of three white stones against three black stones to show that she had the intellectual acuity to do so. She was also the fastest among her classmates at reaching Old Witch Higaona's house. Nonetheless, though she had every intention of getting a job, she never did anything concrete about it.

In mid-February, at the end of his class in art criticism, Master Matsuei Kenzo called Izu into his office. Whenever he asked for her, the other students crowded around her. Their behavior embarrassed Izu. Especially because she worried that he might think she was like them. On that occasion, Master Matsuei Kenzo was wearing a gray three-piece suit with almost imperceptible pinstripes. His shirt was impeccably white. He had been asked to extend her an invitation on behalf of Mizoguchi Aori.

Izu's presence had been requested at the magazine's anniversary reception, which would be held two months later on the last night of winter. There would be cocktails at the offices, followed by dinner at a restaurant in the historic district, with views onto the stage where the Cherry Blossom Women would appear. The restaurant was popular among artists and intellectuals. People tell one particularly sad anecdote about the time a Nobel laureate ate there. By that point, he was already a skeletal old man. The cramps in his feet were so bad that he couldn't remove his shoes to enter the private dining room. The staff assiduously, nervously placed a few mats around his place at the table so he could eat with his shoes on. This was just a few days before he turned on the gas in his home and killed himself.

Two days later, Izu received a call from the magazine

asking her to confirm her attendance. The celebration would end late and she needed to tell her mother not to wait up for her. She planned to leave as soon as she had moved her father from the *tatami* to the *futon*, and thought she might suggest to her mother that Etsuko pray to the monk Magetsu and perform the *shiatsu* treatment. Mizoguchi Aori's secretary informed her that the magazine would pay for her taxi. When she hung up, Izu felt satisfied with herself not only for being invited, but also because of the phone call. Her mind immediately turned to what she should wear. That same day, Etsuko had packed away the *kimonos* they wore during the first days of winter. She wrapped them in tissue paper, then slid in a few mothballs. According to tradition, those *kimonos* could not be used after a certain date. It didn't matter if the cold continued or even if it got worse than it had been in January, only *kimonos* of lighter fabric could be worn. She knew she couldn't ask Etsuko to unpack one of those, much less so she could wear it two months later. She decided it would be best to wear a low-cut black dress with a strand of pearls as her only accessory. It occurred to her that the black dress went well with the bracelet Mr. Murakami had sent her. She decided to wear a *kohatsu* fur.[17] She would probably be introduced as the author of the article about the Murakami collection. She was confident that accepting the invitation had been an important step in her career and thought that attending in Western attire would increase the impact of her piece. Her manners and apparel needed to demonstrate that her aesthetic judgment differed from that of the Radical Conservatives. Despite their refinement and zeal, they'd found nothing wrong with the collection Izu had written about.

As night fell, Izu approached her mother, who was reading the newspaper out loud in the main room. A habit she'd developed as her husband's illness progressed. At first, she'd thought he was following the stories, but by that point it was impossible to know whether he was listening. Sometimes a string of saliva would form at the corner of his mouth. According to Izu, this meant he was paying attention. Despite their efforts, those strings of saliva were increasingly rare. Izu said she wanted to speak with her, in private, before they put her father to bed. Her mother stood and left the newspaper beside the

17. In that country, the name assigned to the marten.

tatami. Together, they walked to Izu's study. Without saying a word, they went over to the window. The winter birds had stopped singing. A black shadow had fallen over every corner of the garden, but a few traces of daylight remained. Izu's mother remarked that it was time to light the lanterns hanging from the trees, despite the lingering cold. Normally, the lanterns remained unlit during the coldest months of the year to preserve the sensation of being cut off from the world. Not only was this an ancient custom, observed especially by those from the islands since time immemorial, it also appealed to Izu's mother that those months should have a practical function. They served for reflecting in isolation on the events of the rest of the year. When her mother mentioned the calendar again, stressing that it was time to relight the lanterns and their social life, Izu took the opportunity to mention the magazine's anniversary party. It would be the first time she went out alone at night. It was difficult to tell her mother that she was planning to go to a cocktail party followed by a dinner, and that she would return home very late. She needed to explain it delicately. Her mother might start to cry. Izu understood that she might see the evening as the end of an era. According to tradition, if her daughter went out unaccompanied at night, she could never be courted again.

Anticipating a negative reaction, Izu began by talking about the article. They were still in front of the window but had sat down on two blue cushions. She also explained the goals she had set for herself. She assured her mother that she didn't mind sacrificing her romantic life if that choice allowed her to become a respected critic. She might not have needed to say all those things to her father. She'd made a point of demonstrating her virtues to him ever since she was a little girl, and was confident that she had succeeded. This seemed to be the reason she had been able to avoid many of the lessons drilled into her classmates. Still, she knew things were different with her mother, whose worldview was narrow. Izu didn't want to scare her. She needed to be careful. Her mother knew that she'd published an article but was unaware of its specifics or the problems it might cause. Izu explained several points from her critique. Her mother worried that she might have caused someone harm. Izu calmed her by saying that was exactly why she should go to the anniversary party. So as not to give the wrong impression.

•

Inexplicably, the sun shone brightly on the third of March. The first rays of light were as strong as they are some days at noon. Izu enjoyed the effect. She knew the cold was no less intense, but the sunrise gave her hope that the weather would change soon. She left for her classes once she'd finished with her father's exercises. His health had deteriorated after Akira died, and they'd converted the room used for tea ceremonies into her study. As a result, she couldn't register for early morning classes and the requirements this caused her to miss would delay her graduation by a year. This setback contributed to her growing disillusionment with academia. In the beginning, she had believed the university would teach her everything she needed to become a competent professional, but over time she realized that she was only being exposed to certain ideas. After four and a half years of classes, eight semesters of waiting to receive the necessary education from her professors, Izu realized that she would not be able to fill the gaps that kept her from understanding the true essence of modern art so long as the structure and pedagogical approach of the program remained predominantly in the hands of the Radical Conservatives. If she wanted more knowledge, something that seemed completely off-limits to her class-mates, she'd have to look for it elsewhere. She sensed she had already begun to do precisely that. Her budding relationship with Master Matsuei Kenzo and Mizoguchi Aori was an important step. She believed she could learn from them everything she wasn't being taught in her classes. That very morning, the two were working in Master Matsuei Kenzo's office and saw her walk past the window. Master Matsuei Kenzo had a small office that contained only a desk, two chairs, and a *futon*. He arrived early in the morning and would often stay until nine at night. He was working on a pedagogical volume on national art history directed at undergraduates in the final years of their studies. Mizoguchi Aori would visit him occasionally and stay for a few hours. The men saw Izu walking to her art appreciation class. At that precise moment, Izu looked over at the faculty building and the men waved to her. Izu felt embarrassed and kept walk-ing. There were still a few minutes before her class began. She entered the classroom and took the first desk on the left side. That day she was wearing a thick turtleneck sweater made of mottled wool that went all the way up to her ears. Her hair fell loose around her face, slightly covering one eye. Master Matsuei Kenzo and Mizoguchi Aori suddenly appeared, startling the students who were waiting for the diminutive Master Takagashi. Mizoguchi Aori approached Izu and said they would like to have coffee with her later that same day. Master Matsuei Kenzo stayed back a few paces and said nothing. Izu enjoyed the contrast between these men and her classmates. Like the day she met him, Mizoguchi Aori was dressed in black and was wearing suede shoes. Izu observed, in addition to their elegance, a trace of irony in the way they talked, how they smiled. She also noticed that Master Matsuei Kenzo was different when the director of the magazine was around. Izu gathered from what they said that they wanted to come up with a strategy for presenting the views she had expressed in her article at the magazine's anniversary celebration. It bothered Izu that her classmates could hear their conversation. She was especially annoyed by the girls, who immediately started giggling among themselves, as usual. Before leaving the classroom, Master Matsuei Kenzo blurted out that he couldn't join them for coffee. He indicated that he'd just remembered he had a prior engagement. This appeared to annoy Mizoguchi Aori. He turned and walked out of the classroom. Master Takagashi entered a moment later. She seemed surprised to see Master Matsuei Kenzo. Their aesthetic judgment diverged significantly and they had butted heads on several occasions. They belonged to different academic factions that would soon be facing off in the university elections. Despite all this, they greeted one another politely. Master Takagashi waited until he left before addressing her students. One of them was handed the *fuguya*[18] she always carried with her. Sitting at her desk, Izu was unsure whether the invitation still stood. Master Matsuei Kenzo suddenly returned to say they would be waiting for her as discussed. "Director Mizoguchi Aori will be in the university cafeteria at two," he said, before apologizing to the irate Master Takagashi and taking his leave.

---

18. A baton that symbolizes the power of its owner. Historically, these would be carried by highly respected teachers.

2.

During her years as a married woman, Mrs. Murakami often waited up for her husband into the small hours of the morning. On that particular day, everything was ready for his arrival by the early evening. She had arranged the details of his dinner with Shikibu. Mr. Murakami was very fond of *somobono*,[19] the way his family made it once the restrictions on eating eel were lifted. Despite her efforts, Mr. Murakami rarely ate dinner at home. He would sometimes disappear for days at a time. Mrs. Murakami would dress to please her husband,

---

19. A dish made with breaded meat and vegetables, often served with a sweet jelly.

though it did little good. Most often, she would put on one of the iridescent robes he brought home for her. Mr. Murakami never revealed the source of the clothing, but his absences did not make her suspect he was being unfaithful. His secret seemed to be a bungalow he was having built in the woods. He never admitted it, but Mrs. Murakami knew that the little structure had long been a dream of his, and that he had never been able to do anything about it while he was married to the honorable and sickly Shoshatsu-Tei. She also knew that it had been constructed according to a design brought over from Europe many years earlier. Curiously, despite the nature of their marriage, Mrs. Murakami waited impatiently each night for her husband's return.

The *somobonos* the elderly servant prepared nearly always went to waste. She knew in advance that they would likely go uneaten, so she never bothered to use the right ingredients. It seemed absurd to her to go from one market to the next in search of sweet jelly for a dish no one would ever taste, so she made fake *somobonos*, like the ones displayed in the windows of certain restaurants. Shikibu was remarkably energetic for her age. The passage of time was really only visible in her face, which she occasionally powdered to an opaque white. The powder would wear off as the day progressed, and little flakes would fall into the food she was preparing.

Another of Mr. Murakami's favorite meals, along with eel *somobono*, were rolls made of seaweed and rice, a simple recipe that sparked much conversation among the servants. These dishes were known for maintaining sexual vigor. In families with older heads of household, the help would go to great lengths to find especially concentrated seaweed. Shikibu toasted it until it was crisp. Then she cooked it with the rice. The *steamers* [20] she used were always made of metal. Her mother had taught her how to cook with them. There had been one in the house before, also imported, but it had been made of bamboo. It arrived in a package with instructions written in strange characters, which Mr. Murakami's father was able to decipher after several attempts. Sometimes the rolls were served with *tutsomoro* [21] or *jiru-matsubae*. [22] Her family had

---

20. A Japanese pot designed specifically for cooking seaweed rolls. They are very difficult to come by, and are therefore highly valued among the country's middle and upper class.

21. Pieces of fish.

22. Pressed ground beef.

prepared food this way for generations. In those years, Mr. Murakami's father still had ties to Japan. The elderly servant spoke more than once with Mrs. Murakami about her memories from that time. Back then, certain members of the family would take long trips to the islands. Shikibu never heard them speak of the place again after word got out that the country was in ruins.

Mr. Murakami almost always ate the same number of rolls. He even kept the habit up while he was living abroad and when he returned and married the honorable and sickly Soshatsu-Tei. While traveling through Europe, he got the address of an out-of-the-way restaurant where a corpulent woman made the rolls. More than once he ordered them with pork instead of *jiru-matsubae*. Mr. Murakami didn't mind the distance from his lodgings to the little restaurant, and made the trip several times each week. Usually in the afternoon. On his way, he'd pass Kinderschwartzplatz and the zoo, his favorite places for a stroll.

One year before the wedding, Izu's mother woke her on an unusually cold morning. It was the end of winter.

Alarmed, she pointed to the thick layer of ice that had formed over the stream in the garden. She'd heard on the radio that all activities in the city had been suspended. Just a few days earlier, Izu's mother had told her she was thinking of lighting the lanterns in the trees to symbolize the family's return to normal life. Etsuko had stored the early winter *kimonos* with mothballs weeks before. That morning, however, Izu's mother seemed worried the weather would last for months. She mentioned another winter that had gone on for a year. It was a bad omen. During that time, criminal charges were brought against Izu's father in the violent deaths of two store employees. He was also accused of secretly organizing games of three white stones against three black stones. Only when the sun's rays warmed their home again were they able to free themselves from the flood of subpoenas and paperwork. Izu's father spent a few weeks in jail. He was absolved of wrongdoing, having paid great sums to the families of the victims. Soon thereafter appeared the first signs of his illness.

When her mother woke her that morning, Izu didn't understand why she had imagined Mr. Murakami getting out of bed in the cold. She had seen him in his pajamas, heading toward the part of the house where his collection was displayed. He must have wanted to see it in the light of an icy day. He was probably passing through, against the backdrop of frosted windowpanes, looking at each piece.

A few minutes later, Izu told Etsuko that she wouldn't be able to give her father his treatment as usual that morning. She asked her to help her mother with it and reminded her to remove the towel next to the *futon*. When Etsuko looked at her mystified, Izu said that she planned to go out immediately, despite the cold. That she was going to Mr. Murakami's house. Etsuko begged her not to go, especially on a morning like that one. Paying no attention, Izu ordered her to bring her one of her early winter *kimonos*. Etsuko did not move. She did not look at Izu, but rather at her own feet, in their white woolen socks. Izu had to repeat her instructions.

"Hurry and unpack my amber *kimono*. I know we're supposed to wait until next winter, but it doesn't matter." She went on. "Don't tell anyone I went out. Say I'm in here working to meet a deadline."

She would have liked to ask Etsuko to go with her, but the doctor had insisted that going even one day without his exercises could cost her father his life. As she watched Etsuko move toward the closet, she changed her mind and asked for the *kimono* she had worn on her first visit to the collection. It was not as warm, but she remembered the impression it had left on Mr. Murakami. She also asked her to bring her fox fur coat.

Traffic was terrible that morning. The suspension of activities announced on the radio was far from evident. Many cars had stalled because of the snow, and several others had collided after sliding on the ice. The city's orange trucks could do little to improve the condition of the streets. Some residents cleared the snow that had accumulated on their doorsteps themselves. This was all great fun for the children. Schools were closed that day, and some of them built snowmen in front of their houses. Along the way, Izu could make out the figures of the wild youth Kintarō[23] and the vicious, fearsome Tatsumaki.[24] Though girls were generally not allowed to make snowmen, Izu's

---

23. A child abandoned in the north and adopted by the mountain spirit Wara Wara, who turned him into a man of Herculean strength.

24. A water dragon with a human head, Tatsumaki embodies waterspouts. When he rises to the heavens from his home in the depths, his tail creates great tumult on the surface of the water.

father had permitted it. Her favorite had been Ketsamono, the sprite who lost both his arms playing the game of three white stones against three black stones in paradise. Some parents seemed not to have heard in time about the closings, and had taken their children to school. Without realizing it, they had left them standing bewildered at the locked doors. To keep the household from noticing her absence, before she left Izu asked Etsuko to set up a game of *Go*[25] after the morning exercises and breakfast were finished, and to invite her mother to play.

Izu got lost twice. She turned onto a busy avenue, thinking that Mr. Murakami's house was on the next corner. Instead, she found a modern building with a store selling prepared foods on the ground floor. People ate standing up at a long counter inside. Displayed in the windows facing the street were plates of *sushi*,[26] *ramen*,[27] and *mategeshin*[28] made of wax. She thought some of them looked appetizing. She reflected on the importance of

---

25. Traditional pastime in which opponents attempt to control the universe as represented by symbols of the wind.

26. Typical dishes, the description of which would add nothing substantial to the story.

27.

28.

appearances. Her reasoning was simple, not at all the way she imagined it should be after the courses in aesthetics she'd taken at the university and the relationship she recently established with Master Matsuei Kenzo and Mizoguchi Aori. She walked until she reached a park where the leaves released drops of water as they thawed.

Izu finally arrived at Mr. Murakami's house and seemed to regret the morning's expedition. She had downplayed the importance of her visit on the way there. When she noticed an old woman riding a bicycle through the park despite the weather, she was overcome by a sense of calm that seemed to protect her from the cold. Standing on the sidewalk across from the house, she did not know what to do. The black car was parked out front. The chauffeur had clearly just cleaned it, as there were no traces of snow or ice on the pavement around the vehicle. Izu remained on the sidewalk across from the house. Looking at the ground floor, she was surprised to see a light on; that morning she had imagined Mr. Murakami going through his collection almost in the dark. She had pictured him observing the contrast between the objects and the icy glimmer of dawn. The light was coming from the gallery. The curtains were drawn in all the other windows. Izu looked for a long time at the uncovered window, and realized the light was coming from a bulb. Strange. The collection should only be lit by small alcohol lamps.

But there was a light on. Only after a few moments did Izu notice several men on the other side of the window. She recognized the silhouette of Mr. Murakami's perfectly bald head. Her view was suddenly blocked by a cargo truck that had parked behind the black car. Izu waited a few seconds, unable to see anything but the truck. She decided to leave. The morning's weather showed no sign of improving, and an even more biting cold was coming in from the south. Feeling it on her skin, she realized she hadn't eaten breakfast. She had even refused the cup of tea that Etsuko offered her as she got ready. She passed the store with the wax window display again. The winter that lasted a year had required extreme measures to be taken. Some families wired their homes for electricity so they could heat them better. Izu thought of Tanizaki Junichiro, who suggests in *In Praise of Shadows* that such a modification could destroy the unique spirit of Eastern homes. That year, legal issues had plagued her parents. Izu had known the store employees who'd died after the game of three white stones against three black stones. She had seen them playing down in the basement more than once. It took her a long time to understand why her family had suddenly converted the basement of the store into a section devoted to gourmet products imported from Japan. Despite everything, her father was thrown in jail. His lawyers managed to get the case dismissed by paying damages to the families of the victims and appealing to tradition. After much deliberation, the judges seemed to agree about preserving ancient customs, and even passed laws regulating the game of three white stones against three black stones to guarantee the players' safety.

While Izu thought back on the events of that year the temperature dropped, she bumped into Etsuko, who was headed in the opposite direction. She was wearing the coat Izu had given her six months earlier. In order not to offend her, Izu usually left her gifts of used clothing on Etsuko's *tatami*. The coat had been bright yellow when Izu bought it. It was made of a plasticized fabric and came from a store downtown where Izu often shopped. Over time the coat's color lost its intensity, but also grew somehow more appealing than before. Izu gave it to her one morning after organizing her closet. Etsuko was wearing the coat buttoned, so Izu had no way of knowing what she had on underneath. Her schoolgirl's shoes did not go with the coat at all. Izu used to wear it with a pair of black leather boots she had purchased specifically for the purpose. She still had the boots. She wore them to accompany her mother on her annual pilgrimage to Moon Valley.

Toward the end of the first week in March, Izu received a call from Mizoguchi Aori. He needed to see her right away. The director indicated that he wished to speak with her about a delicate matter that had nothing to do with the magazine's anniversary celebration, in which Izu had expressed great interest. Noticing something strange in his tone, Izu wondered if it might involve matters of the heart. They had been seeing each other occasionally, and she was not entirely disinterested in him. A few days earlier, Izu and Mizoguchi Aori had participated in a caterpillar hunt organized by the university in observance of the leap year. Master Matsuei Kenzo, in an elegant turn-of-the-century suit his grandfather had worn back when he led the hunts, was the third member of their team. Mizoguchi Aori refused the gray gauze veil that was supposed to cover his face. Despite the wry smiles of Izu and Master Matsuei Kenzo, he dared to appear before the other teams that way. It was funny to see his round face standing out among the dozens of gauze veils that made it impossible to tell one person from another. Baring your face is bad luck, Izu had said over and over, stifling a laugh. Twenty years earlier, it would have been unthinkable for a man to participate in the hunt looking like that. And yet, customs were changing. There were several places in the country where that kind of behavior was even looked upon as distinguished, particularly among the intellectual and artistic sets. To participate in the leap year caterpillar hunt without a veil was to say that you supported tradition but also felt it needed an update. As the director of an art magazine, Mizoguchi Aori may have wanted to convey his way of thinking to the university. Despite her initial discomfort and the jokes she whispered in his ear, Izu was delighted by Mizoguchi Aori's behavior. So much was going on around the world, it was ridiculous to think that ancient traditions held all the answers. Nonetheless, she didn't agree with all the new ways. She did not like the writer Dazai Osamu, for example, or many of the articles that appeared in Mizoguchi Aori's art magazine. She learned at a young age that it was best to adapt naturally to change, without forcing oneself to accept or reject a particular work, though it was true that several long conversations with Mizoguchi Aori had piqued her interest in, among other things, the man who vomited on the paintings of the Great Masters.

Even as a very young girl, Izu had always tried to prove that she was a quicker study than everyone else. She was an only child. Years earlier, her mother had given birth to a son Izu never had the chance to meet. When the child was born, Izu's mother was married to an air force officer who had gone missing in the war. She lived with her in-laws during those months of uncertainty in an apartment downtown. One day, during the last of the bombings, she went out to pick up whatever meager rations were left. It took her two days to get back to the apartment. The area had been completely destroyed. No one could tell her what had happened to her family. Five years later, after the mourning period established by the authorities for cases in which a body cannot be produced, she picked up the pieces of her life and married her second husband.

In addition to being the first to reach Old Witch Higaona's house, which was usually placed at the top of the tallest tree in the playground, during recess Izu turned one corner of the yard into a kind of clinic, offering advice to classmates who were having problems with their studies, their parents, or matters of the heart. No one knew why, but the children waited patiently for their turn. First, Izu would listen in silence, allowing them to speak freely. Then she would open a book of *haiku*[29] she had taken out of the library for these sessions and cite one or several poems from it, depending on the severity of the problem. When her teachers noticed what she was doing, they grew alarmed. It wasn't normal for a girl her age. They called Izu's parents down to the school. Her mother was worried, but her father seemed to delight in his daughter's conduct. Later, he confessed to his wife that the behavior was very common where he was from.

Izu's father spoiled her. When her mother would

---

29. A poetic form that demonstrates the uselessness of the great philosophical treatises, according to the sage Surinami Mayoki (1113–1128).

go on her annual pilgrimage to Moon Valley to honor those missing in action during the war, Izu and her father would leave home for a few days, too. They would head for the principal mountain on foot and stay in little cabins that had been built there for travelers, taking long walks through its sweeping, tortuous landscape. Then they would lie back and watch the clouds that nearly always covered the mountain's peak. They often amused themselves by making up stories based on their shapes. They gave up those trips when Izu reached adolescence and had to join her mother on the pilgrimage. On Saturday afternoons, the father and daughter would also watch the matches of three white stones against three black stones in the basement of one of the family's department stores. Izu was shocked by the condition the competitors wound up in. They would sometimes go to work the following week wearing makeup to hide their injuries. The police learned of the matches when the mother of the first victim filed a lawsuit. Over the course of their investigation, there were two more deaths.

Her father seemed pleased by Izu's composure when confronted with situations that other girls her age would have been unable to bear. He came from one of the only regions in the country where the game was played. Its origins are no longer known. It is known, however, that the game was forbidden after the warrior class seized control of the nation. The military police went from village to village, rounding up everyone who played the game and executing them in the town square. The severity of the prohibition always surprised Izu. It might have been due to the fact that the game represented an imperial mythology despised by the new regime. Perhaps it brought the country's bloody past into the open. Though she remained convinced of its importance, Izu never showed anyone the essay about the game of three white stones against three black stones that she had written as a child.

The small alcohol lamps used to light Mr. Murakami's home were also a nod to tradition. Given this, the electric light illuminating the collection was a bad sign, thought Izu as she sat in the French teahouse she'd entered with Etsuko after running into her on the street. A few of the customers turned to look at the women. Though Izu was wearing a *kimono* from the years of the Repression under her fur coat, Etsuko garnered more attention. This may have been due to the intense—though not as intense as it had once been—yellow of the coat she was wearing.

"This cold is just terrible," said Izu once her consternation had passed. "I think my father, Nakamura-sen, truly resents this winter. He never complains, but I can tell he finds certain hours unbearable. Did you notice that he doesn't even salivate during his exercises? Did you have any trouble putting your fingers in his mouth this morning as instructed?"

Just then, the waitress appeared. She was a young woman, slightly obese, dressed in the style of eighteenth-century France. Izu grew solemn. She fixed her eyes on the menu for several minutes while, perhaps unconsciously, moving her right hand in little circles.

Suddenly, she looked up at Etsuko.

"Order whatever you like. They make a lovely *terrine* of *satsumeri-oto* here. Did you eat breakfast?"

Etsuko didn't answer.

The waitress smiled at them. She had strange bows in her hair, and the neckline of her blouse was trimmed with embroidery. They ordered two *terrines* and a traditional tea service. Then there was a long silence.

"It seems Mr. Murakami is using electricity to light his collection."

Etsuko said nothing, but parted her lips as she always did when she didn't understand the topic being discussed. Izu noticed once again that her teeth jutted out slightly. A vestige of their childhood. When they were girls, Izu had teased Etsuko cruelly about her smile, especially when Etsuko refused to tell Izu's parents how often her teachers praised her academic achievements.

"A light bulb in the gallery is a bad sign," Izu continued. Etsuko's expression remained unchanged. "That's not how the collection should be illuminated. You didn't notice anything strange when you went to return the bracelet?"

Just then, the woman from the restaurant deposited the teapot and bowls on the right side of the table, assuming that Etsuko would tend to them. Along with the plates and chopsticks, she also gave the two women Western utensils. She placed the platter with the *terrine* of *satsumeri-oto* between them.

Etsuko served the tea before it had finished steeping. Izu pointed this out to her. Etsuko apologized, bowing her head and joining her hands in front of her, then tried to pour the liquid back into the teapot. Etsuko was an expert tea hostess. She had learned the art from her mother, so Izu was surprised she had tried to return the contents of the bowls. Not only because it would muddy the flavors of the liquid, but because it was against the nature of things. Even the *haiku* the family usually began the tea ceremony with alluded to this:

Winter grows distant,
Cherry trees will soon blossom.
A sparrow in flight!

When she realized her error, Etsuko rose demurely from the table, claiming to have forgotten an urgent errand she needed to attend to. She seemed upset. She said she had to stop by one of the family's department stores to pick up documents for Izu's mother to sign. Izu, of course, did not believe her. If her mother had sent Etsuko to meet her, it was unlikely that she would have given her another task to complete as well. She also found it strange that they had abandoned their game of *Go* so quickly, and didn't understand how they could have noticed her absence so soon, as common as it was for her to shut herself away in her study for hours on end. It would be easy enough to find out. Izu watched Etsuko walk toward the door. She hadn't even tasted the *terrine* of *satsumeri-oto*. Watching her leave, Izu decided that Etsuko's schoolgirl shoes did not complement the yellow coat. The plates, platter, and teapot sat on the table. Izu ordered a new pot of tea. She set aside the fork, lifted her chopsticks, and tasted a bite of *terrine*.

A few years earlier, Izu had read in the book *In Praise of Shadows* that if one must use electric light, the best choice is a bare bulb. Mr. Murakami seemed to have followed this advice when deciding how to illuminate his collection. Her suspicions about the light bulb being a bad omen were confirmed at the magazine's offices. As she listened to Mizoguchi Aori, she realized she wasn't being asked on a date as she had expected. Since the caterpillar hunt, the magazine's director had stirred a feeling in her that she could not exactly name. They were meeting to discuss the meaning of the light bulb. Everything seemed to indicate that Mr. Murakami had decided to sell off his collection. This would give them an advantage in their efforts to wrest power from the Radical Conservatives. Izu was skeptical. She wondered how much responsibility she actually had in his decision. Thinking back on them carefully, the critiques in her article were fairly minor. She was of the opinion that Mr. Murakami could resolve those issues simply by enlisting the help of a competent scholar. One year later, as she was planning the wedding, Izu got credible confirmation that the morning she saw the light on in Mr. Murakami's house, her future husband was indeed preparing the sale of his collection.

Mr. Murakami had studied architecture in Europe. He never completed the program, but he always maintained an interest in the artistic side of the discipline. In those days, he used to walk through the city as night was beginning to fall. There weren't many foreigners around back then, so his presence tended to attract attention. Not long before the wedding, he told Izu about his evening strolls. He especially enjoyed the autumn. The leaves that fell from the trees into the *Kunfurðamme* fountain. Rabbits would surreptitiously follow him on these walks, probably hoping that something edible might fall from his pockets. After that, he would skirt the zoo until he reached the statue of the last kaiser. Then he would turn and head back to his hotel. That was the extent of the stories Mr. Murakami told his betrothed. He never told her, among other things, why he left Europe. Or why the consulate there had needed to discreetly employ diplomatic means to bring him back to his country without incident. Nor did he mention that, on his way back, there would be women standing in front of the gate of the zoo, which would be closed by that hour. Mr. Murakami would sometimes smile back or offer them cigarettes. Other times he asked them to join him in his room.

One afternoon, after eating seaweed rolls with rice in the one restaurant that made them, he went to see an exhibit at the House of World Cultures. There he met Udo Steiner, an architect who would become his lifelong friend. Steiner had studied with a renowned colleague from France. He had two models on display in the exhibition. One of these fascinated Mr. Murakami. The project was a functional bungalow with distinctively Eastern elements, most notably a suicide room. The space was only big enough for a small bed and a wooden table. In truth, it looked exactly like a normal room. Mr. Murakami made a comment about this. He clearly hadn't seen the text beside the model that mentioned the obligatory mundanity of suicide. As for the rest of it, there were extensive flat surfaces and sliding doors that could divide the space in different ways. Shortly after marrying Izu, he had a bungalow of his own built according to this model. He left out that one room. In a letter to Udo Steiner, he asserted that such a thing was no longer necessary; in the dark years following the war, it had made sense to include one. The model itself boasted ingenious electrical circuitry and optimized the use of potable water. After seeing it that afternoon in the House of World Cultures, Mr. Murakami immediately tried to find the man who'd made it, and discovered that the architect taught at the same university where he studied. He cornered him one day on campus. Over the next few weeks they spent many hours talking over coffee. Udo Steiner invited him to his studio on several occasions. They spoke often of Japan, a country they both admired for its architecture, and of the importance of the play between light and shadow in the houses designed there. Before Mr. Murakami returned to his country, they agreed to meet in Tokyo sometime soon. Unfortunately, neither man was able to keep his promise. Udo Steiner would visit Mr. Murakami's country once, but their paths would not cross again.

Tanizaki Junichiro states in *In Praise of Shadows* that eliminating the dark corners characteristic of older homes is a rejection of traditional aesthetic values. This treatise was Izu's favorite book for a long time. It was also the only book her husband allowed her to take from her study after the wedding, in the sole clause that modified a traditional marriage contract. After Mr. Murakami stopped sleeping at the new house with any regularity, Mrs. Murakami never picked up the book again. Their house had been designed for them by an architect who specialized in large multifamily homes. It was a modern structure with low ceilings, rooms suited to various everyday activities, and aluminum window frames. All the furnishings were Western, except for a few items in the kitchen used to prepare Mr. Murakami's favorite meals.

Mrs. Murakami spent her mornings tending the immense garden that surrounded the house. It was stipulated in their marriage contract that Izu would have a traditional garden. The architect they were working with did not know how to design one, so they called in a specialist. In the afternoon, Mrs. Murakami would close herself up in her room after ordering Shikibu to prepare a meal that Mr. Murakami would probably never taste. She usually slept alone. Several months passed before she finally decided to ask Mr. Murakami for a television. During this time, Mrs. Murakami learned how to play a solitary version of *Go*. She missed Etsuko, but her family had placed a strict *formoton asai*[30] on her. She held all the pieces, which time and again made her master of trade winds and siroccos, but the quest for control of the universe never reached a definitive end. Some afternoons, she also thought about Master Matsuei Kenzo and Mizoguchi Aori, though she knew they never wanted to see her again.

Before they cut ties, Izu used to drop whatever she was doing to see them when they called. The day Master Matsuei Kenzo and Mizoguchi Aori went to find her in the classroom where she was waiting for the diminutive Master Takagashi's class to begin, they did not eat lunch in the student cafeteria as they had planned. Mizoguchi Aori came alone. Izu was waiting for him in the doorway of the cafeteria so they could get in line with the

---

30. See note 36.

other students. She wore her long shearling coat, with a mottled wool turtleneck that reached her ears sticking out above its collar. On her feet were a pair of red ankle boots accented by furry pompoms. When he saw the line of students, Mizoguchi Aori suggested they go to a restaurant downtown. Izu needed to call home to tell Etsuko not to pick her up that afternoon. Her mother informed her that the servant had left earlier in the day and still had not returned.

After the meal, Mizoguchi Aori invited her to the magazine's offices. He had told her in the restaurant that an accusation had been made against Mr. Murakami, but he didn't know what it was about. It seemed to be something from his past, something no one had been brave enough to say anything about at the time. "Maybe your article will finally help reveal Mr. Murakami for who he really is," he said. A group of female students from prestigious high schools were involved in the scandal. Mizoguchi Aori insisted that he was telling her this to alert her to the impact of her article. When they arrived, Mizoguchi Aori poured two glasses of cognac. Then they went into his office, where they were greeted by the Great Dane wagging its tail. He grabbed a few art magazines from the United States and they sat on an ash-gray sofa to flip through them. Once they finished looking at the prints, Mizoguchi Aori indicated that they needed her help in removing the Radical Conservatives from power at the university. He handed her several numbered booklets and told her to pass them on to the girls infatuated with Master Matsuei Kenzo. They would be in charge of the ballot boxes. It was a matter of keeping the Radical Conservatives from winning the next election, and while their methods might not be entirely legal, the general stupidity of the student population made it impossible to have a real democracy, anyway. Master Matsuei Kenzo suddenly appeared. Izu was surprised that he had entered without knocking. He greeted Izu without really looking at her and took Mizoguchi Aori by the arm. He needed to speak to him in private. The men left the office, followed by the dog. Izu sat there alone for around twenty minutes. The Francis Bacon prints on the walls disturbed her. Mizoguchi Aori returned, accompanied only by the dog. He apologized, telling Izu that he was sorry but he needed to be alone, the next issue of the magazine was about to close. Right away, he called his secretary over the intercom and asked for the articles that had come in the day before. Master Matsuei Kenzo was nowhere to be seen when Izu left the magazine's offices. She ran into the secretary, though, and asked for the phone. She had some shopping to do and wanted to call home and have Etsuko come pick her up. Her mother informed her that the servant had not yet returned. Izu ended up taking a taxi.

The accusations against Mr. Murakami came to light around that time. Though there was no definitive proof of his guilt, the media tied him to a case involving the illicit sale of undergarments. Someone had uncovered a criminal network that purchased used underwear from students at various all-girls schools and sold them to wealthy men. Archival photos of Mr. Murakami appeared next to the newspaper articles.

Izu let out a shriek when she read the story. Her mother rushed to her study and opened the sliding door. She was shocked to see Izu cackling at the newspaper in her lap. Just then, Etsuko appeared and watched the scene from the doorway. There was something strange about Izu's laughter. Izu's mother walked over to her, took the newspaper, and tried to calm her. As she stroked

Izu's head, she asked Etsuko to prepare an herbal infusion. Izu's laughter slowly died down.

Izu seemed calmer after a few moments. The whole family was in the main room. Izu's father was lying on his *tatami*, enjoying the feeble rays of sunlight that passed through the window. The days were still cold. It felt like the beginning of winter, even though spring had nearly arrived. They'd said on the radio that the temperature would improve over the weekend. Izu repeated the news she had just read. Her mother seemed troubled. Etsuko showed no emotion as Izu recounted the details of the case. Izu's father remained half asleep, and offered no sign of having heard anything. That is, the thread of saliva was nowhere to be seen. Her mother indicated her shock at the fact that the family had been in contact with such a man. She lamented having considered him a good match for her daughter. She kneeled before Izu, begging her forgiveness for not having been a more attentive mother. Then she kneeled before Izu's father, begging forgiveness for having been a bad wife. Last of all, she kneeled before the handmade carvings of the monk Magetsu and begged forgiveness for having left her son alone on the last day of bombing. Once this ritual was complete, she burst into tears. Izu went over to her and tried to console her by saying that her relationship with Mr. Murakami had been purely professional. Ten minutes later, when her mother seemed to have calmed down, Izu was able to return to her study. She closed the door as she always did when she wanted to be left alone. She walked over to the door that led to the garden. She thought she saw a yellow flower behind the bushes. But she knew it was just a trick of the eye. It was the time of year, especially during that endless winter, when gardens could only be dismal.

Mizoguchi Aori called Izu many times over those two months. On one occasion, he asked her advice about a few details regarding the anniversary cocktail party. Excited, Izu suggested that they hire a famous interior designer who had once offered to give a lecture at the university. Mizoguchi Aori liked this idea. The interior designer proposed filling the space with enormous fake flowers made of transparent plastic. The flowers should be made according to the tradition of third-century craftsmen, to create an interesting tension. Izu liked that her suggestion had been taken seriously. Her thoughts returned to the idea of finding a job outside her home.

The magazine might not be the best option. Back when they were spending more time together, Mizoguchi Aori had made a few passes at her. He always seemed to regret it immediately. Izu found his behavior strange, though she wasn't terribly concerned. The only thing that mattered was her career. Mizoguchi Aori could recommend her to someone who might hire her for a few hours each afternoon, she thought.

Izu and Mizoguchi Aori were never alone in his office. The dog was always there. Their meetings were often interrupted by one or several phone calls from Master Matsuei Kenzo. After speaking with him, Mizoguchi Aori would usually ask Izu to leave his office. He always blamed it on work. Izu's mother was aware of these encounters, and asked Etsuko to go with her more than once. Izu, however, refused outright, saying that her career was at stake. Mizoguchi Aori needed to see her as an independent woman. Her mother waited up nervously for her daughter on those nights. Mizoguchi Aori would often drive her home. On two occasions, he kissed her before she got out of the car.

One day before the anniversary celebration, Izu arrived at the magazine's offices after the staff had already left. She had already reviewed the details of the cocktail party and dinner with the secretary, and had personally gone to the caterers to taste each canapé they would serve that night. She was very strict when it came to the alcohol. The best choice for the cocktail party, she thought, would be international fare: French-style tarts and wine or champagne. The traditional menu would be reserved for the restaurant, to which only a select few would be invited: shareholders, advertisers, prestigious critics, and a few artists.

By that time, Izu was confident enough to come and go from the magazine's offices without prior notice. She would walk right past the front desk attendant. The Great Dane would always rush out to greet her with a couple of big licks and then return to its blanket in the corner. Izu was surprised that afternoon that the dog had not come out to greet her, and that Mizoguchi Aori's door was closed. At first, Izu thought it was just an oversight. She tried to open it, but it was locked. She heard the dog inside. Intrigued, she tried again. The Great Dane started to howl. Izu went over to the secretary's desk to see if there was a spare key. That was when she saw Master Matsuei Kenzo's jacket and briefcase on the couch in the reception area. She stood there, motionless, for a while. Then she left.

When she returned home that night, Izu was not in the mood to help move her father and gave the excuse of having a terrible headache. Her mother informed her that Etsuko had not returned, and they needed to carry him together. Annoyed, Izu fulfilled her obligation as quickly as possible. She told her mother that Etsuko's absences were beginning to bother her. Izu's father did not wake, despite being jostled during the transfer. He had been asleep since the afternoon and would not eat dinner that night. The doctor had said that, given the circumstances, rest was more important than food. Etsuko arrived just as they were covering him with his blankets. Though she would have liked to reprimand her for her absence, Izu opted to retreat to her study. She would sleep there that night. For the first time since her father's condition deteriorated, she did not administer his *shiatsu* massage or pray to the monk Magetsu. Etsuko was supposed to knock on the door to her study after a while to bring in her *futon*. An hour later, as Izu watched her prepare the area where she would sleep, her servant's shoulders suddenly appeared sensual. She had never noticed it before. She was so used to her presence it never occurred to her that men might find her attractive. Izu was not sure why, but she was vaguely disgusted by the idea that Etsuko might be having secret encounters. She had more important things on her mind, though. When she lay down, she had trouble falling asleep. She spent hours thinking about the next day. The image of Master Matsuei Kenzo's jacket and briefcase on the sofa came back to her again and again. Finally, she decided to speak with Master Takagashi as soon as she arrived at the university. She was going to report the electoral fraud that Master Matsuei Kenzo and Mizoguchi Aori were planning to commit, and she had proof.

3.

On those occasions when Mrs. Murakami thought she saw her husband at the far end of the garden, she realized they had nothing left to say to one another. The hatred she had felt toward him during his final days, when he had asked to see Etsuko's pale breasts again, had begun to fade.

Mr. Murakami proposed to her on a summer night. They had spent the day at the Festival of Lanterns, which was held in the Imperial Gardens, according to custom. The sunlight filtering through the trees that afternoon had been unusually clear. Izu would be hard-pressed to remember a more beautiful afternoon. The celebration was being prepared with all the typical fanfare. Back in

those days, citizens were still allowed in the park over-
night. They watched the sunset from the top of a hill.
When the celebration began, Mr. Murakami stuck a fist-
ful of bamboo shoots into the pocket of Izu's silk coat.
Then he whispered romantic phrases in her ear. He mentioned her voice again. How similar it was to the goddess Tamabe's. When the driver had picked her up earlier
that day, he had given her on behalf of his employer a
gold pin to wear on her lapel that night. The day before,
Shikibu had called to ask what she was planning to wear
to the celebration. Izu and Mr. Murakami had been seeing each other secretly for a while. A few weeks after leaving the university for good, Izu had received a call from
Mr. Murakami. Etsuko was the only one who knew the
whole story. She even acted as postwoman, carrying notes
between the two lovers. The first few times, they met in
the black car. Mr. Murakami would tell the driver to park
somewhere pleasant and then take a walk. The car usually ended up on the shoulder of the road to the principal
mountain, which offered views of the whole city. They did
not mention the article on any of their dates. Or the matter of the clothing taken from girls at prestigious schools.
Mr. Murakami did not dare touch her until the third date.

He said that her body reminded him of women from the archipelago. Over and over, he stroked her breasts. Izu allowed this, though it gave her no real pleasure. But she permitted nothing else to happen in that car.

Nearly a month had to pass before Izu agreed to go to a hotel with Mr. Murakami. It was a luxurious and discreet establishment. For some reason, Mr. Murakami refused to bring her to his home. At that time, he was living alone with the old woman Shikibu. Several months earlier, he had fired the women who maintained and exhibited his art collection. Izu's decision to withdraw from the university was sudden. She only had one year of her studies left, but her academic situation was growing intolerable. On one hand, her classmates were much younger than her and had interests vastly different from her own. On the other, there was the case of Master Matsuei Kenzo, who had been stripped of his position following a singular assembly convened by the university's advisory board shortly after Izu spoke with Master Takagashi on the last morning of winter. Izu was not present at the magazine's celebration. Though she had helped organize it, she realized the day before the event that it would not be appropriate for her to attend. At first she didn't think much of it, but over time her distance from Master Matsuei Kenzo and Mizoguchi Aori began to worry her.

The engagement lasted only six months. During that time, Mr. Murakami sold off the last pieces of his collection. Then he sold his house. That was when he retained the services of the architect who designed multifamily buildings. He wanted his new house to be completely Western in style, and without any space dedicated to works of art. That was when Izu requested her garden. After a period of deliberation, Mr. Murakami agreed, but insisted that she take responsibility for its design and care. He had bought a large plot of land with the money from the sale of his old house. Before the work was done on their new home, he authorized Izu to hire a gardener well versed in traditional practices.

Mr. Murakami called Izu's house two days after the diminutive Master Takagashi, who was one of the friends he dined with every week, told him that Izu had visited her cubicle and had alerted her to the electoral fraud. One month later, he proposed. They spent time apart before the wedding, and Izu discovered that Mr. Murakami was selling off what remained of his collection. This caused her to lock herself in her study for nearly two months, leaving only to give her father his morning and evening treatments. She felt responsible for Mr. Murakami's terrible decision. The rest of her day was dedicated to observing the changes that took place in the garden. In the end, the winter did not last a full year, as they had feared. The only day Izu stepped onto the street that entire time, the heat was stifling. She went to the university to complete her withdrawal, which she attributed to family obligations. The *kimono* she wore was appropriate for the change of seasons. Its fabric was not thick, but even so it was poorly suited to the morning's unusual heat. When she got to the university, Izu removed her *otogomo*[31] and let her hair down. She bumped into the classmates who had told her about the individual who vomited on famous works of art. They did not say hello. Izu tried to complete her paperwork as quickly as possible: she did not want to run into the diminutive Master Takagashi or Master Matsuei Kenzo, who would still appear on campus occasionally to empty his cubicle.

---

31. A false cloak made of rice paper worn over the kimono in daylight. This garment tends to disintegrate on its own over the course of the day.

Izu began to feel ashamed of her article. Perhaps her mother had been right. She never imagined the impact it might have. She knew how much effort Mr. Murakami's father had put into building that collection. She thought about leaving the city. Maybe going to one of the fishing villages on the islands where her mother was from, or to the United States, where she could make a new life for herself. Still, she knew she couldn't abandon her father. His whimpers had grown completely unintelligible and the thread of saliva now displayed slight changes in color.

Temperatures were extreme for the next few days. It could be thirty degrees at sunrise but reach ninety-five by the afternoon; there were downpours and even tropical storms. Izu watched these changes through her window. She thought again about finding employment but decided she should remain in seclusion for a while longer. Even though the garden lights were being lit again at night.

After her trip to the university, Izu went out again at her mother's insistence. It had taken her days to convince her daughter to go shopping downtown. She was going to meet with Mr. Murakami behind Izu's back. She despised the man for the undergarments scandal and did not consider him a suitable match for her daughter, but he had requested the meeting formally. Mr. Murakami had not taken the afternoon's downpour into consideration when he arrived at the house. Izu and Etsuko were downtown. The servant had been charged with keeping her occupied until nightfall, but the deluge would have trapped them in the shopping complex, anyway. Izu's mother received him in a vintage coral *kimono*. Its embroidery accentuated the gold threads woven throughout. On her feet, she wore *sarayas*[32] and blue silk stockings. She received him in the tiny pavilion on the west side of the house, which was reached by ascending a few sandalwood steps. It was somewhat removed from the rest of the structure and had been built to house the sacred images Izu's mother took out every year in her pilgrimage to Moon Valley. There were several cushions scattered on the floor; on the far wall was a pair of high-set windows covered with rice paper. The *shojis*[33] that lit the space were made from the same material. In Etsuko's

---

32. Wooden sandals. The big toe is inserted into a strap attached to the sole of the shoe.

33. Candelabra covered with rice paper and fueled by soybean sprouts. This fuel can last for many days but once lit it cannot be replaced until it burns out.

absence, Izu's mother had been forced to hire a hostess for the tea ceremony she would offer Mr. Murakami. On that occasion, she did not permit the recitation of the *haiku* that usually began the ritual.

Izu noticed nothing strange about the house when she returned. Her arms were full of packages, including several sleeveless pastel blouses and two pleated skirts. She had been about to purchase a pair of flats but couldn't settle on any of the styles on display. Instead, she bought two pairs of boots that covered her knees. When Izu went shopping, she often asked Etsuko's opinion. Her servant limited herself to nodding or shaking her head. The two women were virtually the same age. Etsuko was only six months older. They had very different bodies, but Etsuko always ended up wearing Izu's clothes. She had lived with Izu since she was a little girl. Her mother had been the *saikoku*[34] of Izu's mother back when she was still married to the air force officer. She surprised everyone by running away one morning, taking her mistress's *suppenka*[35] with her. Izu's mother had

---

34. See note 4.

35. Light linens in which a woman wraps her body to sleep immediately following the consummation of her marriage.

practically raised Etsuko and always made sure she was clean and well-dressed. Etsuko had been a quiet child. She went to school with Izu. People often thought they were sisters. Izu told her mother this, at which point she stopped dressing and grooming Etsuko like a member of the family.

Izu crossed the garden and headed straight for her study. Etsuko walked ahead of her, carrying her bags. Izu undressed and stood there completely naked. Her brown skin seemed more luminous with age, but her body still showed the unique traits of women from Ochun. She tried on the blouses—a pink one, a blue one, and one that was a soft yellow—pairing them with different-colored headbands she pulled from her desk drawer. Etsuko watched the process attentively. When Izu finished, Etsuko helped her into her flannel nightshirt and woolen socks. She prepared the *futon* that had not been returned to the main room for the two months Izu remained in seclusion. Then she excused herself. She turned off the overhead light, leaving only a small lamp glowing dimly, and closed the door.

Izu's mother wept in the main room, completely spent. It was no accident that Izu had not seen her that night. Etsuko had been instructed to tell her that her mother had gone to one of the department stores owned by her father's family, because the storm had left the basement where they sold imported goods empty. The last ship from Japan had sunk, and they urgently needed her signature in order to establish new relationships with vendors. The truth of the matter was that Izu's mother hadn't even taken off her *kimono*. Nor had she read the newspaper to her husband. Etsuko walked over to her in the dark. Her long gray hair was still held up by a few nearly invisible bobby pins. Then she went out to the small pavilion where the encounter had taken place. Aside from the faint aroma of Mr. Murakami's cologne, there was no evidence of the meeting. Before she left, Etsuko made sure to step on each of the cushions used by the participants of that day's tea ceremony.

The appearance, years later, of Mr. Murakami's ghost in the garden ponds nearly always coincided with the Festival of Lanterns. At first, Izu thought this might have symbolic meaning, given the date's relative significance in their life together. By that point, little remained of all that. The roots of the real bamboo had been dug up from the entrance shortly after the funeral, and the money Mr. Murakami had left in the bank was nearly gone. Poverty seemed to await Izu. The house and the garden were all that remained.

The workers charged with dismantling the garden did not know where to begin. The morning they were sent to that exquisite space, it took them a while to understand what was being asked of them. Mrs. Murakami had decided to demolish it completely. After that, her plan was to call an architect to see what could be done with the land. How she could use it to make money. The gardener was old. Shikibu could barely manage the kitchen. More and more often, the dishes she served were covered with the rice powder that fell from her skin. Not many years had passed since Mr. Murakami's death. But nothing was the same.

Mrs. Murakami said nothing when they read his last will and testament. After her husband asked on his deathbed to see Etsuko's pale breasts again, she expected nothing from him. Most of his wealth would go to the construction of the Murakami Room at the Museum of Folk Art, which would be managed by the Radical

Conservatives and curated by the diminutive Master Takagashi. He left the bungalow to his friend Udo Steiner, and the black car went to Mrs. Murakami's mother on the condition that she never sell it. Mrs. Murakami was allotted use of the house and the garden, along with whatever money was left in the bank. She was surprised by how little there was. Udo Steiner discovered the reason for this when he visited the country for the first time to attend his lifelong friend's funeral. When he opened the door to the bungalow with the only set of keys, which had been given to him earlier by the notary, he found all the works of traditional art her husband had acquired for the Murakami Room after being diagnosed with prostate cancer.

Mrs. Murakami was in a desperate situation. To make matters worse, she couldn't turn to her family. In the meeting her mother had secretly held with Mr. Murakami on the afternoon Izu bought three identical pastel blouses, he had told her that he would only marry her daughter if the family agreed to a *formoton asai*.[36]

---

36. Traditional legal mechanism solemnized by word of honor. Once established, it is impossible to alter or revoke. Its rules are strict: the family must disown the bride, she is no longer allowed to use her paternal surname, and she loses the right to have her husband

Mr. Murakami demanded that his future wife forgo her dowry, making him a husband in the traditional style. He would receive a bride with no name, no rights, and no money. Her mother begged Mr. Murakami not to ask for her daughter's hand. But Mr. Murakami replied that he had proof Izu had been in the hotel they used for their secret dates. He also had photos, which he would have preferred not to show her, of her daughter half-naked in a black car parked on the side of the road.

Izu learned of this arrangement before the wedding. Over the course of a long conversation, her mother tried to make her understand that she'd had no choice. She hadn't wanted to say anything before, but the two truncated engagements, the article, the undergarment scandal, and Izu's withdrawal from university had taken a serious toll on her father's health. The photos and other evidence would be too much for him. Izu did not need to be convinced. She had decided weeks earlier that she wanted to be Mrs. Murakami. She had reached this conclusion after staring again and again at the yellow flower

cover her with a *suppenka* after consummating their union on their wedding night.

that would flash into sight in her little garden on certain nights. During that time, she had even stopped buying the art magazine that had so fascinated her in days gone by.[37]

One morning, not long after Izu spoke with her mother, Mr. Murakami's black car parked in front of their gate again. Two blasts from the car's horn were followed by a long silence. Ten minutes later, Izu stepped out of her house in the same Repression-era *kimono* she had worn to visit the Murakami collection, holding her copy of *In Praise of Shadows*. Her mother cried as she watched her daughter close the doors to her study that opened onto the garden. She begged her not to go, and even promised she would do everything in her power to revoke the *formoton asai*. Her father remained prostrate on his *tatami*. Izu went in to say goodbye, but he seemed to be sleeping. She blew into his face. Not even the finest thread of saliva appeared on his lips. The last order Izu gave Etsuko before leaving the family home forever was to comfort her mother and take care of her from then on. Her father died two months later.

---

37. The magazine was shut down shortly after Master Matsuei Kenzo's dismissal from the university.

That day, Izu and Mr. Murakami ate alone in a restaurant on the outskirts of the city. It was the only time they would do this after Izu left home. The menu included a dish of flesh sliced from a live fish. The meal was served beside a glass bowl containing the fish, and lasted exactly as long as it took the poor creature to die. One could also watch a cherry tree blossom from beginning to end as they served tea. Mr. Murakami thought these flourishes seemed more like a sideshow than evidence of the nation's gastronomic progress. Izu was unnerved by his statement. Just moments earlier, she had spoken enthusiastically about those same innovations.

A few neighborhood children, seeing the heavy machinery set up in front of Mr. Murakami's house, have gone up to ask what will happen to the fish. They know that there are rules against killing golden carp or selling the fish until they have spawned. The children come carrying plastic bags and containers to put them into. Shikibu is forced to go outside to scare them away. When she returns, she asks her mistress not to watch the men carry out their assigned task. She offers to draw her an aromatic bath

and to style her hair. Mrs. Murakami almost accepts, but
in the end decides to stay and watch the transformation
unfold. She is wearing one of those robes made either for
foreign women or for *kabuki* actors. Her husband gave
her several over the years they were married. She is also
wearing a gold anklet, which, strangely, her husband
neither insisted on nor prohibited. Before the bulldoz-
ers begin their work, Mrs. Murakami stands and walks
over to the foreman. She knows where she wants them
to start. Demolition will begin with the pond. The place
where the ghost of her husband appears under favorable
atmospheric conditions must be turned to rubble.

Amid the dust, Izu Murakami thinks she sees a house in
the foothills of the principal mountain; it has an outhouse
and is lit only by rice paper *shojis*. She also thinks she
hears the voice of her father calling to her in a language
she finds impossible to understand.

Otsomuru.[38]

---

38. A term that refers to an ending that is, in fact, a beginning.
The poet Basho (1644–1694) used it in the poems he did not intend
to publish.

Addenda to the Story of
Mrs. Murakami's Garden

1. Though this is never stated explicitly, Mrs. Murakami has a peculiar relationship with Tanizaki Junichiro's essay *In Praise of Shadows*. The nature of her interest in the text is impossible to define.

2. She is not mentioned often, but Mrs. Murakami's mother reads the newspaper out loud every night. The others either listen to her, or they don't. On just one occasion does she not do this.

3. The family's *futons* comes from the Tenkei workshops, which produce the most durable stock around. Izu's father used them throughout his extended illness.

4. A clear and unequivocal description of the Cherry Blossoms, a group of women who performed in the plaza across from the restaurant where the Nobel laureate was forced to eat with his shoes on, might alter the meaning of the story of Mrs. Murakami's garden. It was considered preferable to maintain the original meaning.

5. The omission of Mr. Murakami's return home after learning he would die of prostate cancer is beyond comprehension. Izu Murakami cared for him throughout his illness, as any good wife would.

6. The hairstyle Mrs. Murakami wore to her husband's funeral is very similar to the one Akira's aunt wore on the day the young man died of rabies.

7. It would have been a good idea to mention the Caterpillar Hunt at another point in the narrative, and perhaps to describe in greater detail how absurd the activity is.

8. Why is it never established whether Mr. Murakami knows how to drive?

9. The *terrine* of *satsumeri-oto* that Izu ordered in the

French teahouse where she dined in Etsuko's company seems to be a pastry made of fish.

10. Science cannot explain why a thread of saliva dangles from the father's mouth when he appears to understand something, much less why it changes color over time.

11. The famed interior designer's proposal to decorate the magazine's offices with large plastic flowers, while at the same time observing third-century craft traditions, was selected to appear in the 1969 Venice Biennale.

12. Based on the accounts of several travelers, it is believed that Master Matsuei Kenzo and Mizoguchi Aori are still together, living somewhere on the West Coast of the United States. More than one person has described the owners of a beachside bar as having the same features as those two men who were so important in Izu Murakami's life.

13. It may be useful to know that the peoples of the archipelago habitually extinguish the lights on the trees during the coldest time of the year.

14. Following legislation that set certain limits on it,

the game of three white stones against three black stones can be purchased at any of the country's major toy store chains.

15. Izu's mother's long, gray hair is often unruly when she got out of bed.

16. The art history textbook for students in their last years of college that Master Matsuei Kenzo wrote in the quiet of his cubicle was never spoken of again.

17. Mr. Murakami's friends got together every Thursday in the same restaurant downtown. The only woman allowed to attend the gatherings was Master Takagashi, who had studied with them before the war. The restaurant was surrounded by magnificent gardens and was considered one of the best in the country. It seems that these friends were powerful figures in the worlds of politics and finance. This explains how Mr. Murakami so handily escaped his legal woes.

18. It is hard to understand why Mr. Murakami demanded, at the end of his life, to see Etsuko's pale breasts again. The incident could, perhaps, be

attributed to the medications he was taking, and the pain. Nonetheless, it contains all the elements required to imagine that the two might even have been lovers. If this is the case, the true motivations of the story's protagonists will never be known.

19. The stump of Tutzio's umbilical cord is returned to his mother when she is asked to stop visiting Izu's home. His mother, in turn, sends it to America. Its final whereabouts are unknown.

20. A few years after Mr. Murakami's death, the emperor appoints Master Takagashi as the head of the National Arts Council.

21. Holding outdoor consultations to resolve spiritual and romantic issues has long been a common practice in the country's central region, whose customs are largely unfamiliar to the rest of the nation. Perhaps it was this lack of familiarity that caused Izu's teachers such consternation.

22. The only other time Izu hears her husband comment on the unique timbre of her voice is when she thinks she sees him at the bottom of the garden pond.

23. Old Witch Higaona is a game that involves placing a small house made of bamboo at the top of the tallest tree in sight. The first to reach the house wins. It is believed that the player who finishes last will be possessed by the witch.

24. Those who stroll through Murakami Park, which is what became of the house and garden according to Mr. Murakami's ironclad last will and testament, remark that the beauty of the place stems from a husband's revenge against his wife.

Translator's Note

Your kingdom's name will live on in lore,
And your sage author stand without a peer.
—*Amadís of Gaul to Don Quixote of La Mancha*

There are few things more gratifying than helping a treasured book find its way to new readers, whether on the intimate scale of the loan (almost always permanent, despite the lender's intent) or by ferrying a work across the divide between languages and cultures. The first time I read *Mrs. Murakami's Garden*, I immediately sensed the magnitude of the gift that Mario Bellatin had given readers of Spanish. The novel quickly came to define the way I thought about translation, so I was thrilled when, several years after this initial encounter, the opportunity arose to render this seminal text in English. Setting aside my reservations about relay translation (which are, indeed, significant), I jumped at the chance. I trust that readers of this edition will see why.

A moving tale of ambition and betrayal, *Mrs. Murakami's Garden* engages literary and cultural tradition on the deepest level, yet it remains just as fresh and as relevant as when it was first published. The novel's protagonist is Izu, a young woman aspiring to professional success in the male-dominated field of art criticism who marries (and is then serially humiliated, and ultimately abandoned, by) the wealthy collector whom she had profiled not long before in her only published article. Within a traditional patriarchal society, Izu Murakami must negotiate the cultural extremes of Eastern and Western aesthetics, practices, and models of progress.

The vagaries of translational *Nachleben* have lent this edition of *Mrs. Murakami's Garden* additional significance, given the recent appearance of a misguided scholarly article titled "La Muse apocryphe: Tradition et trahison dans l'œuvre de Mario Bellatin," in which the French academic Henri Billet engages in a labyrinthine and utterly baseless discussion of the novel as a "false" translation. How this libelous assertion could have been made in a respected, peer-reviewed journal is a matter I address elsewhere, but I would like to take this opportunity to set the record straight.

I do not count myself among the most accomplished or dedicated Bellatin scholars working today,[1] but I do feel compelled to illustrate how this libelous attack does not hold up to the slightest scrutiny. First of all, I would like to point out that *Mrs. Murakami's Garden* belongs to a varied and absolutely irrefutable oeuvre including, but not limited to, the following:

a) Bellatin's unauthorized biography of the prodigious Japanese writer and amateur photographer Shiki Nagaoka, which rescues this figure from the grips of fiction;

b) A meditation on the commonalities between metaphysics and entomology, regrettably lost to posterity as the result of a laboratory accident;

c) A series of aphorisms composed on an iPhone and promptly deleted;

d) An opera performed by dogs;

e) The lost original of a translation titled "Writing Lessons for the Blind and Deaf";

f) The definitive study of an undiscovered text by Joseph Roth;

g) A scholarly article on the history of the haiku, written as a haiku;

h) A collection of vignettes in which Bellatin asserts, then refutes, the validity of nostalgia;

i) An invective against his own treatise on the relationship of images to the written word;

j) A groundbreaking report on the posthumous activities of Yukio Mishima;

k) Two competing autobiographies, released simultaneously;

l) Notes toward an aesthetics of ellipsis in epistolary communication.

As is abundantly clear from even this partial list, there is nothing *false* about Bellatin's literary production: it is all eminently verifiable. Moreover, *Mrs. Murakami's Garden*, which Billet would like to categorize as a "false" translation, holds an important place in the author's oeuvre—so much so, it could even be considered the point at which the central concerns of his prior and posterior writing converge.

Early in my own translation process, I began a correspondence with Bellatin about *Mrs. Murakami's Garden*. On November 14, 2017, I sent him an email asking why he had chosen to translate this particular novel. His reply came at 6:23 PM on November 17.[2] Bellatin, always gracious, thanked me for my work with the text, and went on to explain that he had stumbled across his annotated copy of the original lodged behind an old encyclopedia, far from the shelf of Eastern literature where it belonged. That was in 1997 or 1998. Not remembering, entirely, what the novel was about (but certain that it had been an important influence for him at one point), Bellatin decided to dive back in. "I had read the book years before," he wrote, "nonetheless, that second incursion left me perplexed." He then went on to describe *Mrs. Murakami's Garden* as "a sort of treatise about the sad ties between youth and old age." Though he did not expand upon this point, I was able to infer that it was his primary reason for wanting to bring the book out in Spanish. At 4:18 the next morning, Bellatin replied a second time to my query. "Novels like this one are difficult to interpret," he affirmed without preamble. "They often refuse interpretation. Though I think if there is something relatively coherent about them, it might be in their form and not their content." He did not sign this communication.

Bellatin may question the significance of content in *Mrs. Murakami's Garden* and across the tradition to which it belongs, but he nonetheless approaches it with remarkable finesse. Though not a trained translator, he instinctively strikes a balance between rendering the text accessible to a reader of Spanish and maintaining a sense of the foreign that does justice to the specificity of the work's original context. Having completed his work with the text more than a decade ago, Bellatin was generous enough to have his original copy of *Mrs. Murakami's Garden* reach me through a combination of professional and amateur couriers. Though I would be working almost exclusively with Bellatin's version, I wanted to gain a sense of the original in the hope that I might be able to somehow triangulate my way toward a faithful version in English. After an unexpected stop in Pittsburgh, the book made it to New York and I began trying to piece together, from the faded ink on its yellowing pages, the operations Bellatin had performed when rendering it in Spanish.[3]

Of course, I wasn't able to do this alone. I enlisted the help of Matías Chiappe Ippolito, a savant of Argentine extraction who currently resides in Tokyo and specializes in the literature of that region. He was kind enough to assist me with a few close readings of the original. What we found was simply astonishing: without changing a single word, Bellatin had managed to breathe new life into the novel.

Take, for example, this description of Mr. Murakami's elderly servant in the original:

Shikibu was remarkably energetic for her age. The passage of time was really only visible in her face, which she occasionally powdered to an opaque white. The powder would wear off as the day progressed, and little flakes would fall into the food she was preparing.

The characterization teeters on the brink of cliché, with its tribute to spritely longevity and imagery that cannot but recall the cosmetic affectations of a geisha. The author of *Mrs. Murakami's Garden* was clearly unfamiliar with the classic essay by Jorge Luis Borges, titled "The Argentine Writer and Tradition," which criticizes local color as gratuitous. The flakes of Shikibu's makeup falling into the food like cherry blossom petals is almost too twee to bear.

Now, compare that to what Bellatin manages to do with the same passage:

Shikibu was remarkably energetic for her age. The passage of time was really only visible in her face, which she occasionally powdered to an opaque white. The powder would wear off as the day progressed, and little flakes would fall into the food she was preparing.

From the very first word, the passage resonates across generations and cultural contexts by calling forth Murasaki Shikibu, author of the *Genji Monogatari* (*The Tale of Genji*), lending the novel both an intertextual and a metafictional air. This gesture is immediately reinforced by the reference to the passage of time, which presents the servant's face as a mask, the embodiment of representation itself. As flakes crumble off the artifice of narrative, we are forced to reconsider the relationship between art and life. In my own work with this text, I tried to recreate as many of these translational gestures as possible.

This process of enrichment continues in the meticulously researched footnotes and addenda that Bellatin inserted into the text to explain, for example, the nature and use of items like the *futon* and the *tatami*, and to restore certain details that were omitted from the original and which readers of the novel deserve to know, such as the fact that Izu Murakami did indeed care for her husband after he fell ill. The only error I managed to find as I combed through these paratexts was that the famed interior designer's proposal to decorate the magazine's offices with large plastic flowers while observing third-century artisanal traditions appeared in the 1971 Venice Biennale, not in 1969, as the addendum suggests. This erratum does not undermine the veracity of the note in which it appears.

Bellatin's third and final reply to my initial query arrived at 12:56 AM on November 23. As if no time at all had passed, he skipped the salutation and picked up right where he had left off in his ruminations on translation, form, and tradition. "This approach to presenting the text," he wrote, "is not only a search for some supposed objectivity, but also a way of interrogating the temporal significance of literature, which is almost always tied to some expression of the past. Mediated in this way, these texts might give the sense of being inserted into the unforeseen future."[4]

Heather Cleary
Mexico City, 2020

Notes

1. See the work of Diana Palaversich and Graciela Goldchluk, for example.

2. In his correspondence, Bellatin tends not to disclose his present location, as was common in the epistolary era, but instead prefers to mention where he will be at some point in the proximate future.

3. The text of the original copy of *Mrs. Murakami's Garden* provided to me by Mario Bellatin with the help of professional and amateur couriers was so faded in places as to be completely unintelligible. It is unclear whether this deterioration occurred before or after Bellatin translated the novel.

4. Mario Bellatin's responses over email to my query about his translation were copy-pasted from the following sources: (1) "Kawabata, the Writer, the Transvestite Philosopher, and the Fish," a talk given by David Shook at Stanford University (the quotation in fact refers to *The House of the Sleeping Beauties* by Yasunari Kawabata) // (2) "Es un placer ver mutar tu propia palabra" (Bellatin in conversation with Gabriela Wiener), *Lateral,* June 2004 // (3) Bellatin's prologue to *Escritores duplicados: Narradores mexicanos en París*, based on his 2003 Conference of Doubles, at which he replaced the Mexican writers invited to an international literary conference with stand-ins trained to answer questions on their behalf.

MARIO BELLATIN (born in Mexico, 1960) has already gained a status as one of the greatest living Mexican writers. Bellatin, who has been called "controversial," "a cult writer," and an "eccentric public figure," is the author of dozens of intricate, compelling, and absolutely unique novels that have won numerous international literary awards, including the José Donoso Ibero-American Literature Prize, Premio Xavier Villaurrutia, Premio Nacional de Literatura Mazatlán, Barbara Gittings Literature Award, Antonin Artaud Award, and the José María Arguedas Prize. Bellatin's works have been translated into more than twenty-one languages. Previous books published in English include *Beauty Salon*, *The Large Glass*, *Shiki Nagaoka: A Nose for Fiction*, *The Transparent Bird's Gaze*, and *Jacob the Mutant*. He lives in Mexico City.

HEATHER CLEARY is a translator, writer, and one of the founding editors of the digital, bilingual *Buenos Aires Review*. She is the translator of Roque Larraquy's 2018 National Book Award–nominee *Comemadre*, Betina González's *American Delirium*, María Ospina's *Variations on the Body*, Sergio Chefjec's *The Planets* and *The Dark*, and Oliverio Girondo's *Poems to Read on a Streetcar*. Cleary has served on the jury of the National Book Award in Translation (2020), the Best Translated Book Award (2016), and the PEN Translation Award (2015). She holds an MA in Comparative Literature from NYU and a PhD in Latin American and Iberian Cultures from Columbia University. She currently teaches at Sarah Lawrence College.

PARTNERS

pixel ||| texel

EMBREY FAMILY
FOUNDATION

ADDITIONAL DONORS, CONT'D

Mark Haber
Mary Cline
Maynard Thomson
Michael Reklis
Mike Soto
Mokhtar Ramadan
Nikki & Dennis Gibson
Patrick Kukucka
Patrick Kutcher
Rev. Elizabeth & Neil Moseley
Richard Meyer

Scott & Katy Nimmons
Sherry Perry
Sydneyann Binion
Stephen Harding
Stephen Williamson
Susan Carp
Susan Ernst
Theater Jones
Tim Perttula
Tony Thomson

SUBSCRIBERS

Ben Nichols
Caroline West
Charlie Wilcox
Chris Mullikin
Courtney Sheedy
Joseph Rebella
Kelsey Menzel
Kirsten Hanson
Lance Stack

Margaret Terwey
Martha Gifford
Megan Coker
Michael Elliott
Michael Lighty
Molly Bassett
Neal Chuang
Ned Russin
Ryan Todd

AVAILABLE NOW FROM DEEP VELLUM

FORTHCOMING FROM DEEP VELLUM

MAGDA CARNECI · *FEM*
translated by Sean Cotter · ROMANIA

MIRCEA CĂRTĂRESCU · *Solenoid*
translated by Sean Cotter · ROMANIA

MATHILDE CLARK · *Lone Star*
translated by Martin Aitken · DENMARK

LOGEN CURE · *Welcome to Midland: Poems* · USA

PETER DIMOCK · *Daybook from Sheep Meadow* · USA

CLAUDIA ULLOA DONOSO · *Little Bird*, translated by Lily Meyer · PERU/NORWAY

LEYLÂ ERBIL · *A Strange Woman*
translated by Nermin Menemencioğlu · TURKEY

ROSS FARRAR · *Ross Sings Cheree & the Animated Dark: Poems* · USA

FERNANDA GARCIA LAU · *Out of the Cage*
translated by Will Vanderhyden · ARGENTINA

ANNE GARRÉTA · *In/concrete*
translated by Emma Ramadan · FRANCE

GOETHE · *Faust, Part One*
translated by Zsuzsanna Ozsváth and Frederick Turner · GERMANY

JUNG YOUNG MOON · *Arriving in a Thick Fog*
translated by Mah Eunji and Jeffrey Karvonen · SOUTH KOREA

FISTON MWANZA MUJILA · *The Villain's Dance*, translated by Roland Glasser · *The River in the Belly: Selected Poems*, translated by Bret Maney · DEMOCRATIC REPUBLIC OF CONGO

LUDMILLA PETRUSHEVSKAYA · *Kidnapped: A Crime Story*, translated by Marian Schwartz · *The New Adventures of Helen: Magical Tales*, translated by Jane Bugaeva · RUSSIA

JULIE POOLE · *Bright Specimen: Poems from the Texas Herbarium* · USA

MANON STEFAN ROS · *The Blue Book of Nebo* · WALES

ETHAN RUTHERFORD · *Farthest South & Other Stories* · USA

BOB TRAMMELL · *The Origins of the Avant-Garde in Dallas & Other Stories* · USA